This Nature Storybook belongs to:

_____

_____

_____

_____

WALKER BOOKS

Once wolves roamed nearly all
the lands of the northern hemisphere.
But they have been hunted and killed
by humans for centuries, and today they
are extinct or very rare in places where
lots of people live, including Europe
and much of North America.

Most wolves now live in the far north
of the world – in Alaska, Siberia, and
parts of Canada such as the Yukon
Territory, where this story is set.

For John, my North Star
J.H.

For William and Daniel
S.F.-D.

First published 1997 by Walker Books Ltd, 87 Vauxhall Walk, London SE11 5HJ

This edition published 2015

2 4 6 8 10 9 7 5 3

This book has been typeset in Weiss and Sanvito

Printed in China

British Library Cataloguing in Publication Data:
a catalogue record for this book is available from the British Library.

ISBN 978-1-4063-6545-0

www.walker.co.uk

Walk with a WOLF

Janni Howker

illustrated by

Sarah Fox-Davies

WALKER BOOKS
AND SUBSIDIARIES
LONDON • BOSTON • SYDNEY • AUCKLAND

Walk with a wolf in the cold air before sunrise.
She moves, quiet as mist,

between spruce trees and birches.
A silent grey shadow, she slides between boulders
and trots over blue pebbles to the edge of the lake.

She plunges through slush ice and laps the chill water,

snaps at a feather that drifts down from a goose wing,

then splashes to shore and

shakes herself like a dog.

Wolves were probably the first large animals to live with people, and all the kinds of dog we know today are descended from them.

There's deep snow on the mountains.

Snow clouds bank in the east.

Winter is coming, and the geese fly south.

Run with a wolf as she bounds up the steep slope.

She sniffs at a skull that stares at the lake.

Moss grows on the antlers.

The bone has turned grey,

there's no meat on it now –

and she's hungry.

During the summer months, a wolf may hunt alone
and catch fish, hare, squirrels and other small animals.
But these creatures go into hiding in winter,
to escape from the freezing cold weather.

Howl with a wolf in the dawn, thin and icy.

Deep from her chest the eerie sound comes.

Long, low music.

The song of the Arctic.

Another howl answers.

With a wag of her tail, the wolf runs to the pack.

Three sons and a daughter, cubs from the spring,

squirm on their bellies and lick at her neck.

Mother wolves give birth in springtime.
They can have anything from one to eleven cubs each year.

Although they don't stay together all the time, most wolves live in family groups called packs.

The black wolf greets her with a stare from his pale eyes.

He's her mate, the pack's strongest hunter —

and he's hungry, too.

The wolf pack is ready.

They set off together, like eight ghost dogs,

silent and stealthy as the coming of frost.

Three ravens are flying high overhead.

Most packs have up to eight wolves in them,

although packs of as many as fifty have sometimes been seen.

Hunt with a wolf on the trail of a bull moose,

following its tracks and

its scent on the ground.

Wolves have to hunt as a pack
if they are to kill large animals,
such as moose and deer.

There's a crash in the bushes – the moose is close.

The wolves crouch on their bellies,

their hearts beating fast.

There's danger in hunting –

a kick from a moose can break a wolf's ribs.

Charge with a wolf!

The pack breaks through the bushes,

swift as grey lightning with one bolt of black.

The moose turns and sees them.

But he's old and he's limping.

There are scars on his legs.

The wolves leap at him, biting.

Hear the moose bellow.

Hear the wolves panting as they drag him down.

Drops of his blood fall like berries to the ground.

Rest with a wolf, no longer hungry,

she watches the cubs come to join in the feast.

If there is plenty of food around, pack members will all feed at once.
But if meat is scarce, the strongest wolves will eat first,
and the youngest, the cubs, last.

25

Sleep with a wolf while a blizzard is blowing.

The sky is full of a million grey ice moths,

as the wind drives the flakes down.

Backs to the gale, the wolves curl among boulders,

heads tucked between hind legs,

and noses covered by the fur of their tails.

Dream with a wolf as the Pole Star is shining.

There's thick snow on the ground and a shivering wind.

But the wolf dreams she is walking

  with new cubs in warm sunlight,

as the wild geese return with the spring to the lake.

Index

cubs 14, 24-25

dogs 8

feeding 25

food 10

howling 12

hunting 10, 18-20, 23

moose 18-19, 22-23

pack 15, 17-18, 25

where wolves live 3

Look up the pages
to find out about all these wolf things.
Don't forget to look at both kinds of word –
this kind and *this kind*.

About the Author

Janni Howker is fascinated by wolves. "The fact
that wolves have been extinct here in Britain for over
200 years should make me feel safe," she says, "but instead
it makes me sad. The sound of wolves howling would
make winter evenings magical."
This is Janni's first picture book for children, but
she is also the award-winning author of the short story
collection *Badger on the Barge*, and the novels
The Nature of the Beast, *Isaac Campion* and *Martin Farrell*.

About the Illustrator

Sarah Fox-Davies hopes that *Walk with a Wolf*
will show readers that "wolves are not the monsters of
folklore. They are wild animals that survive only through
their skill as hunters and their co-operation as a pack."
She has illustrated several picture books for
children, including *Little Caribou*, for which she also wrote
the text, *Little Beaver and the Echo* by Amy MacDonald,
and *Moon Frog: Animal Poems for Young Children*
by Richard Edwards.

Note to Parents

Sharing books with children is one of the best ways to help them learn. And it's one of the best ways they learn to read, too.

Nature Storybooks are beautifully illustrated, award-winning information picture books whose focus on animals has a strong appeal for children. They can be read as stories, revisited and enjoyed again and again, inviting children to become excited about a subject, to think and discover, and to want to find out more.

Each book is an adventure into the real world that broadens children's experience and develops their curiosity and understanding – and that's the best kind of learning there is.

Note to Teachers

Nature Storybooks provide memorable reading experiences for children in Key Stages 1 and 2 (Years 1–4), and also offer many learning opportunities for exploring a topic through words and pictures.

By working with the stories, either individually or together, children can respond to the animal world through a variety of activities, including drawing and painting, role play, talking and writing.

The books provide a rich starting-point for further research and for developing children's knowledge of information genres.

Nature Storybooks support the literacy curriculum in a variety of ways, providing:
- a focus for a whole class topic
- high-quality texts for guided reading
- a resource for the class read-aloud programme
- information texts for the class and school library for developing children's individual reading interests

Find more information on how to use Nature Storybooks in the classroom at
www.walker.co.uk/naturestorybooks

Nature Storybooks support KS 1–2 English and KS 1–2 Science